No Pain, NO WAY!

Holly Huppert

Illustrated by Mark Braught

STECK-VAUGHN
ELEMENTARY · SECONDARY · ADULT · LIBRARY

A Harcourt Company

www.steck-vaughn.com

ISBN 0-7398-5065-2

Copyright © 2003 Steck-Vaughn Company

Power Up! Building Reading Strength is a trademark of
Steck-Vaughn Company.

All rights reserved. No part of the material protected by this
copyright may be reproduced or utilized in any form or by any
means, electronic or mechanical, including photocopying,
recording, or by any information storage and retrieval system,
without permission in writing from the copyright owner. Requests
for permission to make copies of any part of the work should be
mailed to: Copyright Permissions, Steck-Vaughn Company,
P.O. Box 26015, Austin, Texas 78755.

Printed in the United States of America.

2 3 4 5 6 7 8 9 LB 06 05 04 03 02

CONTENTS

Make Me!

The judge said, "Young man, are you listening?"

Jed stared at his hands. He was tired of everyone telling him what to do. He was fifteen years old. He could take care of himself.

His grandmother whispered, "She could send you to jail. What's wrong with you? Is this how I raised you?"

Jed didn't answer. Yes, he stole a car. He didn't hurt anybody. He just liked the thrill. He wondered if the judge knew anything about thrills.

"Jed, I could lock you away. It would give me a thrill to see that look wiped off your face," the judge said.

Jed looked up, but not because he was worried about going to jail. He was surprised that the judge used the word thrill just as he was thinking that word. It was strange. He looked at the judge. Was she a mind reader?

The judge threw up her hands. "Fine. Jed Wilson, I sentence you to sixty hours of community service. It must be done within three months."

Jed's face turned red. The judge said, "You will work at a center for seniors for the next ten Saturdays. Maybe you'll learn something by helping older people." Jed couldn't believe it. The judge wanted him to work on Saturdays for nothing.

His grandmother whispered, "Say something!"

Jed looked at the judge. "What do I have to do there?" he demanded.

"The center is a place where seniors live. Sometimes older people need help. Sometimes they just don't want to live alone. Your job will be to do whatever they need."

Jed stared at the floor. "No pay? No way," he said to himself.

The judge asked, "What did you say?"

"You can't make me work for nothing," Jed answered.

The judge lowered her voice. "Did you say I can't make you?" She shook her head and laughed.

Jed hated to be laughed at. His face got even redder. "Make me," he said.

The judge said, "Okay, I will."

His grandmother started crying. The judge started talking. That's how Jed started working at the center for seniors. ⚡

Every Saturday, a police officer picked Jed up at his house. He drove Jed to work. The police officer always said the same thing. "Where to, work or jail?"

"Jail," Jed would whisper, and the officer would drive him to work.

Fifty seniors lived at the center. Some rode around in wheelchairs. Many took forever to walk down the hall. Jed hated the way everyone bossed him around. Someone was always asking for a drink of water. Others wanted him to find their glasses.

Some people wanted Jed to read letters to them. Jed really wanted to change the letters as he read them aloud. He wanted to fill them with scary stories, but he thought that the judge might find out. She would send him to jail, and that would upset his grandmother. He didn't like to make her worry. So he just read the letters the way they were written.

He hated his job.

Every Saturday afternoon, the officer picked him up. He always said the same thing. "Where to, home or jail?"

"Home," Jed would say. He tried to pretend that he was a rich guy being driven around. It didn't work. He always felt like he was being arrested, again and again.

No Smiles

There was one man at the center named Mack. Jed couldn't stand him. Mack was old, but he didn't have any trouble getting around. His gray hair stuck out all over. It looked like his hair was caught in a windstorm. He always said nice things to people. They seemed to enjoy it. Jed hated it.

One Saturday Jed was sweeping the front porch. Mack walked up to him.

"So, where's your smile? Don't you know that work is easier with a smile?" Mack asked, smiling.

"Fine. You do it." Jed gave the broom to Mack. To Jed's surprise, Mack started sweeping. He whistled and sang as he worked. 𝄢

Jed wondered if he could get Mack to do all of his work. Maybe he could trick all the old people into doing his work. The thought made Jed smile. Mack saw the smile.

"Oh, you did bring your smile. A smile always makes things easier," Mack said.

"I'm not a wimp. I don't need things to be easy," Jed said as he walked away.

The next Saturday, Jed got some bad news. The director of the center said, "Jed, the crafts teacher is sick today. You need to teach a craft."

"Not me," Jed said. "I don't know anything about crafts."

"Jed, you have to. That's your job today. You'll think of something," said the director.

Jed was angry. "You can't make me!" he
yelled. He walked out of the room. He kicked
over a chair. There was no way he was going to
do crafts with old people.

Jed walked into the crafts room. He told everyone there wouldn't be a class. The room filled with low moans. Mack spoke up. "Hey, kid. Can't you do something to entertain us?"

"No way," Jed said. "I'm not a singer." Everyone laughed. Jed was surprised.

Mack spoke again. "Why don't you tell us your story? Why does a police officer bring you to work each week?"

Mack's friend Barbara said, "Tell us. We really do want to know."

Jed glared at them. He never wanted to get old. "Fine," he said. "I'll tell you why I'm here. But first, each of you has to pay me a dollar." ⨎

Chapter 3

The Dollar Story

Jed was only kidding. He didn't think they would do it. Then, they all started pulling dollars out of their pockets. Jed wondered if he could get in trouble for taking their money.

A man sitting near the front said, "This story better be good. And speak up. You mumble too much."

Jed got nervous. He hated speaking in front of people, and these people had paid him. What if he couldn't tell them a good story?

Mack called out, "And we want to hear the truth. Don't make up anything. We only care about what really happened."

14

Jed shrugged his shoulders. He would tell them the truth all right.

"I'm a car thief," he said. "I steal cars. Old cars. New cars. I can take anything with wheels." Jed knew this wasn't exactly the truth. He had only stolen one car, but that wouldn't make a good story.

Everyone had questions. Jed told them to raise their hands and wait to be called on.

"Son, are you even old enough to drive?"

"No, but I know how. My dad used to race cars. When he was alive, I helped him move them."

Mack looked surprised. "I raced cars. I might have raced against your father."

Before Jed could find out more, someone had another question. "But what do you do with the cars?" Barbara asked.

"Oh, sometimes I just drive around until I run out of gas. Sometimes I pick up my friends and take them for rides."

Mack raised his hand. "Can you steal a car without scratching it or breaking the locks?"

"Of course." Jed smiled. "I have a master key that works on some cars. My father's friend gave it to me. I used it to move race cars around."

"Oh," Mack said. "Do I have a job for you!"

Jed saw the look in Mack's eyes. He knew he should have walked out. Mack was going to ask him to break the law. He could just feel it.

A Bad Idea

Mack asked, "Could you move my son's car when he comes to visit?"

"Why?" Jed asked.

"He used to make fun of me when I couldn't find my car. He told me I was old. I would love to see him trying to find his car. You could just drive his car to the other side of the parking lot. He wouldn't be able to find it. I could tell him he was old."

Everyone in the room started laughing. Then they started asking Jed to move their kids' cars. Jed held up his hand for quiet.

Everyone stopped talking. He was surprised that they obeyed him. "Now, why do you want to make your kids mad? Maybe they won't come to visit you if you do."

The room was quiet. Mack said, "They don't come to visit often. But there is a special lunch in two weeks. They will all be here. Oh, it sure would be a funny thing to see!"

Two weeks from now would be Jed's last Saturday. He walked back and forth across the room. It was hard to think when there were twenty people staring at him. He told them that he would think about it.

The day of the big lunch finally came. Jed felt in his pocket for the key. His father would have been upset that Jed was using the key to steal cars.

It was time to start. Jed waited until all of the visitors were inside with their parents. He used the key to open a car door, and in seconds, the car was running. Quickly and easily, he moved the car into the back parking lot.

Next, Jed jumped into a fancy, red car. The car started right up. He moved it to the side parking lot and chose his next car.

He was having fun. He loved being part of the joke on the families. He couldn't wait to see what happened.

Jed had just moved his last car when he saw someone coming toward him. "No way," he said.

Standing Alone

The police officer who drove Jed to work every day was watching. He had seen everything. He grabbed Jed and handcuffed him. He took Jed's master key and said, "Oh, the judge will love to see this." The other officer pushed Jed into the back of the police car.

"I should have known you would never make it here," the officer said. "Stealing cars again? You have the right to remain silent. Anything you say can and will be used against you."

Jed cut in, "Man, this was all a joke. The people who live here asked me to do it."

The officers wouldn't listen.

Jed yelled from the back seat, "Hey, officer. You forgot to ask me if I wanted to go home!"

The officers didn't answer him.

Two days later, Jed was back in court. This time, he was alone. Jed was scared. He might go to jail. That's why he wouldn't let his grandmother come with him. He didn't want her to watch him get sent to jail. He had to get out of this himself.

The judge shook her head. "Jed, I can't believe it. You are still stealing cars. You haven't learned anything, have you?"

"Yes," he said. Jed knew he only had one chance to tell his story.

"This is terrible," said the judge. "I want the truth. Start talking."

Jed began. "Do you know what it's like for the people at the center? Nobody ever comes to visit them. And when they do come, it's only for a few minutes. The seniors just want someone to write a letter for them. Or they just want to talk for awhile. I feel sorry for them." ⚡

The judge nodded.

"Well," Jed said, "I wanted to help Mack and Barbara and their friends. They wanted to play a trick on their kids. They wanted their kids to stay longer. If their kids had a good time, maybe they would visit more often. It was my last Saturday. I had a special key. I just moved a few cars from one side of the parking lot to the other. I didn't steal anything."

The judge crossed her arms. "You still took something that didn't belong to you. That's not okay," she said.

Jed was afraid he would start to cry, so he kept talking. "The kids couldn't find their cars. The old people thought it was funny. The kids thought it was funny, too. They all went back inside to have more coffee. Everyone laughed."

Mack had called to tell him about it. Mack said he would come to court, but Jed wouldn't let him.

Jed said, "I know it was wrong. But don't you believe me? I just wanted to make everyone happy."

The judge did believe Jed. She knew he had changed. This wasn't the same young man who'd been in her court before. But Jed had done something wrong. She had to do something.

The judge asked, "What do you think I should do? You stole a car. I sentenced you to community service. Then, you stole cars again. What should I do with you now?"

Jed said, "Maybe you could make me work at the center again?"

"I don't think so," the judge said. "I don't think they would want you back. You broke the law. No, this time, you'll pick up trash in the park."

Jed couldn't believe it. He really did want to go back to the center. He wanted to ask Mack about car racing. Did Mack know his father? "What if they will take me back? Can I work there instead of the park?" Jed asked.

The judge was quiet for a long time. "Yes. But I need to see a letter from the director. The letter must say they want you back. But if I see you again, we'll be talking about jail. Do you understand?" ⸮

"Yes, ma'am, I do," Jed said.

When court was over, Jed ran all the way home. He told his grandmother he had more community service to do. Then he got out a piece of paper and a pen.

Dear Director,

I'm sorry I broke the law. It was wrong. I really do want to work at the center again. Could I come back? Things will be different. I will even teach crafts. I would also like to spend more time with Mack, if you don't mind. I promise I will follow all of the rules.

Please let me know.

Thanks,

Jed

Dear Jed,

When can you start?